BJ climbed into the tow truck,
and away they went
down the road.

The farmer was waiting for them
by the gate.
"Follow me," he said.

"You are just in time," the farmer said.
"The water is coming up fast.
My best cow is down in a ditch,
and I can't get her out
with the tractor."

BJ and Toby
followed the farmer.
They went down the farm track
to the ditch.

"She's down there," called the farmer,
and Toby stopped.

“We will have to back up
to the ditch, Toby,” said BJ.
“That’s it! Now stop!”

“Moo-oo-oo,” said the cow.

BJ jumped down
from the tow truck.
Then the farmer helped him
put two big straps
around his best cow.

"Take her up slowly, Toby,"
shouted BJ.
"That's it! Good!"

The cow came up
out of the muddy ditch.
"Moo-oo-oo," she said.

BJ climbed back into the tow truck.
Toby started to move,
but his wheels began to spin.

The wheels went round and round
and round in the mud.
BJ pulled on the brakes.

"Moo-oo-oo," said the cow.

"Tell the farmer to get something
to put under my back wheels,"
said Toby to BJ.
"I can't move on this wet ground.
It's too muddy."

The farmer went up the hill
to the shed.
He came back
with some straw
and some old sacks.

BJ slid the straw and the sacks under Toby's wheels.

"Now, let's try again," he said. "Come on, Toby."

V-room, v-room, v-room!
Toby began to move slowly across the muddy ground and up onto the farm track.

"Thanks for saving my best cow,"
said the farmer.

"There was nothing to it," said BJ.
"It was all in a day's work."

Toby and BJ

Story by Annette Smith

Illustrations by Craig Smith

"Come on, Toby," said BJ
to his tow truck, one wet day.
"We have to go to River Road Farm.
We have to get a cow out of a ditch."